SESAME STREET

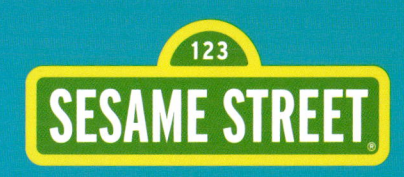

WELCOME TO GERMANY WITH SESAME STREET

CHRISTY PETERSON

Lerner Publications ◆ Minneapolis

In this series, *Sesame Street* characters help readers learn about other countries' people, cultures, landscapes, and more. These books connect friends around the world while giving readers new tools to become smarter, kinder friends. Pack your bags and take a fun-filled look at your world with your funny, furry friends from *Sesame Street*.

—Sincerely, the Editors at Sesame Street

TABLE OF CONTENTS

Welcome to Germany!................. 4

Where in the World Is Germany?........ 6

Germany Fast Facts......................... 21
Glossary 22
Learn More................................. 23
Index 24

WELCOME TO GERMANY!

Germany is a country in Europe.

Hallo! That means "hello" in German. My name is Finchen. I live in Germany. It has lots of amazing castles!

There are many things that make Germany unique. There are lots of things that are familiar too!

WHERE IN THE WORLD IS GERMANY?

Germany and Surrounding Area

SWEDEN
DENMARK
NORTH SEA
BALTIC SEA
NETHERLANDS
Berlin ★
POLAND
BELGIUM
GERMANY
LUXEMBOURG
CZECH REPUBLIC
FRANCE
AUSTRIA
SWITZERLAND

Miles
0 50 100
0 50 100 150
Kilometers

NORTH AMERICA
ATLANTIC OCEAN
PACIFIC OCEAN
SOUTH AMERICA

ARCTIC OCEAN

Germany

EUROPE

ASIA

PACIFIC OCEAN

AFRICA

INDIAN OCEAN

AUSTRALIA

SOUTHERN OCEAN

Germany has green fields and forests. Southern Germany has rolling hills and tall mountains. In the north, there are long stretches of coastline.

The Alps is the highest mountain range in Europe. It stretches through Germany, Italy, Austria, and more!

> Look at all the wonderful people for me to count! Ah, ah, ah!

Many Germans live in cities. Some Germans live in small towns or on farms.

In December, some German towns have Christmas markets. Shoppers can buy food, like sausages. They can also buy gifts, such as handmade ornaments and mugs.

The ornaments are so beautiful!

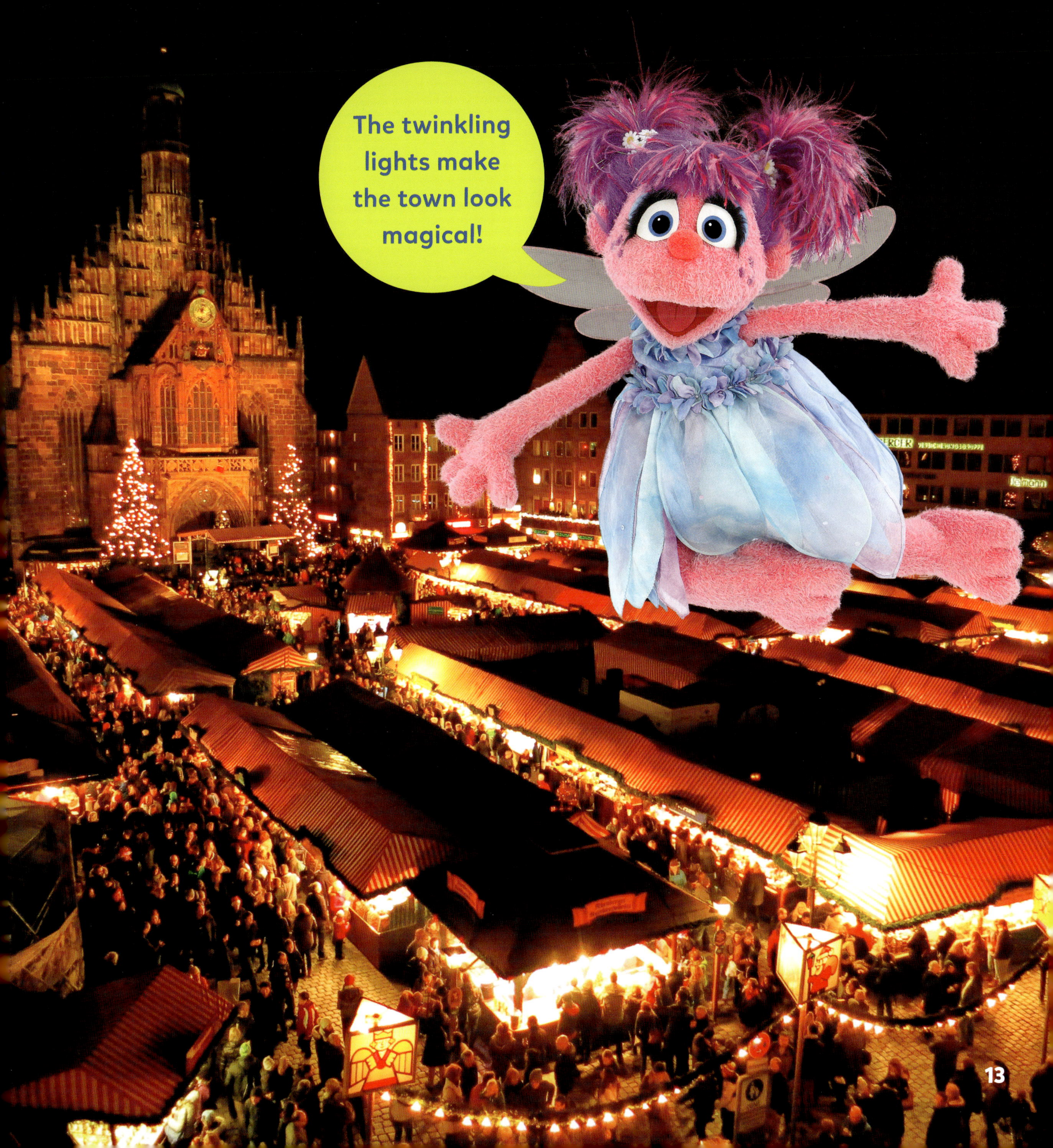
The twinkling lights make the town look magical!

Bread is an important food in Germany.

Me like cookies, but bread good too! *Om nom!*

There are more than 3,000 different kinds of bread!

In Germany, the first day of first grade has a special celebration. Kids get paper cones called *Schultüten*. They are filled with gifts, including pencils, erasers, and snacks.

The first day of school is a big party. Elmo loves parties!

Many Germans like to spend time outdoors. They hike or spend time in their gardens.

"Our garden is very small."

"Cornflowers and edelweiss are two popular flowers in Germany."

"My family likes to play board games. How do you spend time with your family?"

Families in Germany are a lot like yours. They play games and have fun together.

Flag of Germany

GERMANY FAST FACTS

Continent: Europe

Capital city: Berlin

Population: 83 million

Language: German

GLOSSARY

celebration: a party or event held to honor a special person or day

hike: to take a long walk in nature

market: a place where people buy and sell things

mountain range: a line of mountains connected by high ground

ornament: a decoration that traditionally hangs on a Christmas tree

Schultüten: paper cones filled with presents that children receive on the first day of school

LEARN MORE

Bailey, R. J. *Meals in Germany*. Minneapolis: Bullfrog Books, 2017.

Blevins, Wiley. *Follow Me around Germany*. New York: Children's Press, 2018.

Press, J. P. *Welcome to German with Sesame Street*. Minneapolis: Lerner Publications, 2020.

INDEX

bread, 14

hike, 18

market, 12

mountain, 8–9

school, 17

Photo Acknowledgments

Image credits: Valerio Bruscianelli/Wikimedia Commons (CC BY-SA 4.0), pp. 4–5; Laura Westlund/Independent Picture Service, pp. 6–7, 21; MWolf89/Wikimedia Commons (CC BY-SA 4.0), p. 8; canadastock/Shutterstock.com, p. 9; leoks/Shutterstock.com, p. 10; Sina Ettmer Photography/Shutterstock.com, p. 11; AnjaDuda/Shutterstock.com, p. 12; Dmitry Kovba/Shutterstock.com, p. 13; YesPhotographers/Shutterstock.com, p. 15; Kittyfly/Shutterstock.com, p. 16; Romrodphoto/Shutterstock.com, p. 17; Tom Werner/DigitalVision/Getty Images, p. 18; Timofey Zadvornov/Shutterstock.com, p. 19; David Prado Perucha/Shutterstock.com, p. 20.

Cover: Romrodphoto/Shutterstock.com (top); Boris Stroujko/Shutterstock.com (bottom).

Copyright © 2022 Sesame Workshop,® Sesame Street,® and associated characters, trademarks and design elements are owned and licensed by Sesame Workshop.

All rights reserved. International copyright secured. No part of this book may be reproduced, stored in a retrieval system, or transmitted in any form or by any means—electronic, mechanical, photocopying, recording, or otherwise—without the prior written permission of Lerner Publishing Group, Inc., except for the inclusion of brief quotations in an acknowledged review.

Lerner Publications Company
An imprint of Lerner Publishing Group, Inc.
241 First Avenue North
Minneapolis, MN 55401 USA

For reading levels and more information, look up this title at www.lernerbooks.com.

Main body text set in Mikado a Regular.
Typeface provided by HVD Fonts.

Editor: Andrea Nelson
Lerner team: Martha Kranes

Library of Congress Cataloging-in-Publication Data

Names: Peterson, Christy, author.
Title: Welcome to Germany with Sesame Street / Christy Peterson.
  Description: Minneapolis : Lerner Publications, 2022. | Series: Sesame street friends around the world | Includes bibliographical references and index. | Audience: Ages 4–8 | Audience: Grades K–1 | Summary: "The European country of Germany has green fields, tall mountains, and a mild climate. Readers travel to Germany with their Sesame Street friends to learn about German families, food, festivals, and more"— Provided by publisher.
Identifiers: LCCN 2020040569 (print) | LCCN 2020040570 (ebook) | ISBN 9781728424385 (library binding) | ISBN 9781728430485 (ebook)
Subjects: LCSH: Germany—Juvenile literature. | Germany—Social life and customs—Juvenile literature.
  Classification: LCC DD17 .P46 2022 (print) | LCC DD17 (ebook) | DDC 943—dc23

LC record available at https://lccn.loc.gov/2020040569
LC ebook record available at https://lccn.loc.gov/2020040570

Manufactured in the United States of America
1-49308-49424-1/6/2021